BRAVE
THE PLANE
WHO WAS AFRAID TO FLY

By Fiona Reid

_____

Presented To: ....

From: ....

Date: ....

Thank you to my Late Mother Clover Reid.

Thank you to my Grandma Esmine and all my family members. Love you all!

Thank you to Pastor Greg and Tamara Dumas, and The Crossing Church.
You are my family!

Thank you to those who have helped in the development of this book:
Joe Kerr, Sally Reid, Jennifer Uhlarik, Chad Hall and Barbara Bode.

Special thank you to the Illustrator: Aliosa Tran Phan.

For more information about the author go to or ⬛f /FionaInspired

"Fiona and I served together at Metro World Child in New York City, during which time I was able to witness her passion for children. Reading Fiona's new book Brave, The Plane Who Was Afraid to Fly was for me an accurate reflection of her heart, as it provides a platform to engage in conversation with children on the relevant topic of fear. It's an easy read with far-reaching benefits."

- Abbigail Rioux, former Education and Training Director at Metro World Child

"Fiona Reid is a gifted communicator with a passion to see children reach their full potential and fulfil their dreams. In her new book Brave, The Plane Who Was Afraid To Fly, Fiona skillfully delivers a crippling blow to every child's worst enemy: The Spirit of Fear. This book will speak to every child that opens its pages. It comes with my highest recommendations."

- Michael Ekwulugo, Senior Pastor, Transformation Life Centre, Birmingham UK

"Brave the Plane is an engaging story that provides entertainment along with practical tools to open up discussion with young children to overcome fear. This book is a must have for parents of small children and teachers!"

- Richard and Kimberly Wilson, Executive Directors, Watchmen Arise International, Inc.

"As a public-school teacher of 11 years, I've seen how fear takes its toll on young people. Unfortunately, many times parents don't know how to start difficult conversations with their children, and this leaves them to find answers elsewhere. That's the beauty of this story: it opens up an important conversation through a fun, inspiring story that is deeper than it appears. Brave's courage shows children they too can be brave!"

- Philip Rivera, Migrant Resource Teacher, Hillsborough County Public Schools

"Children are our greatest future resource in the Kingdom of Heaven, and Satan's greatest enemy. We would be foolish to think that he wouldn't want to discourage them, by trying to get them to live in fear at a very young age. Mixed with fun antidotes and cute turns, Brave is a beautifully illustrated story about dealing with fear the right way. Dad leads the way. Those who are supposed to lead the way do so, demonstrating the power of modeling. In the end, everyone is free! Much of what is currently lacking in Western Christianity can be traced back to the loss of Power, Love and a Sound Mind, and it's never too early to begin to address the spirit of fear."

- Greg Dumas, Lead Pastor, The Crossing Church

"Fear is something we all encounter at some point in our lives. How we choose to respond to fear will either keep us on the ground, stuck going nowhere or propel us to fly as a overcomer doing the impossible. In Brave, Fiona Reid has challenged us all to not be afraid of what we experience, but to how to be a confidant overcomer in our own lives and in the lives of others. Well done Fiona, Well done!"

- Chad Hall, Executive Pastor, Illuminate Church

Introduction

Fear is something all children face. But some are controlled by fear, and if it's left un-dealt with, that fear can affect them into their adult life. The purpose of this book is to help expose where fear may have come in and the lie that is holding your child in fear. Before we begin, let us open up in prayer.

"Father God, I thank You, for Your word says according to 2 Timothy 1:7, "For God has not given us a spirit of fear, but of power and of love and of a sound mind." So today I ask You to come and expose where fear has come in and the lie that is holding (name of child) in fear and show (name of child) Your truth.
In Jesus' name, AMEN."

In the beautiful Highlands of Scotland, you can explore the beautiful castles.

You can jump on a steam train ...*Choo! Choo!* And travel through the mountains and the valleys.

You can canoe or swim across the many lakes, and if you are brave enough, you may adventure climbing the tallest mountain in the Highlands of Scotland - beautiful Mount MacBay.

For hundreds of years, this mountain has been home to one of the most famous airplane families, the MacBay family. Dad Irvine, Mom Bonnie, and their five children:
Annabella 11, Ernest 9, Hilda 8, Flora 7 and Brave 5.

Irvine MacBay, who loved children, started a school to teach children how to fly. He wanted them to be confident in the air. He taught hundreds of planes how to take off, land, and do tricks in the air so they could be confident fliers.

He was the best teacher in town; and they awarded him with a captain's jacket that he always wore over his wings.

Irvine loved to teach all his children to fly.

Annabella, first born, loved fashion. She would never leave the house until she was happy with her style. She would hit the runway with sparkly high heel shoes, sparkly glasses, a sparkly leather jacket and a diamond necklace. She was the fashion queen of Mount MacBay.

Ernest is one of the fastest planes in the Highlands of Scotland. He always competes and wins many prizes.

10

COME FLY WITH US!

Many of the other children and parents would laugh at him. They called him, "The plane who is afraid to fly."

13

His family couldn't understand why Brave was so afraid to fly when there were so many in the family who were very confident at flying.

They decided to hold a family meeting.

Brave's mother, Bonnie, came to the meeting in tears.

"Oh, what has become of Brave?" She cried.

"If he is never going to fly, he will become like my brother, Magnus. He never did leave this mountain. We don't see much of him nowadays. Many say he is hiding in a cave, eating worms and grass. What a life. Oh Brave, don't let this be you." she sobbed.

Irvine put his wing around Bonnie and said,

"Calm down love." Then he began to lead the conversation with Brave.

"Brave, come over to Dad."

"Remember you can tell Dad anything. We share with one another our fears. So, has something happened Brave that has made you afraid to fly?"

"Ummm... kinda..." muttered Brave.

"Oh, my goodness." replied Bonnie, already in tears.

"You tell Momma. Who did it, son?

What is their name?

Do I know their mom and dad?

When did this happen?

Was it when your dad and I were on our date night last week at our favorite restaurant, Hoop-De-Who? I knew we shouldn't have gone. We are so selfish. Forgive us, son. Forgive us!"

"Calm down Bonnie." remarked Irvine.

"What happened son? You can always share with Dad."

"Well..." Brave began nervously, "Annabella and Ernest were watching a movie called CRASH. I knew I was too young to see it, but I sneaked in and saw the most horrible thing.

The plane in the movie was a young plane like me. He was flying for the first time, and he crashed. He didn't just crash. He crashed into cow poo.

The whole village had to wear clothespins on their noses for months because the plane smelled so bad, even though he had taken several baths."

"Oh, don't let this be me, Dad! Don't let this be me!"

Brave began to sob uncontrollably.

"It's okay, son." Irvine reassured Brave.

"Dad wouldn't let this happen to you. I will ensure you know all that you need to know before you fly.

It's going to be great."

"Brave, there is something I need to tell you. I said it's important we share our fears. So now is the time I need to share with you what your older siblings know."

"What is it Dad?" whispered Brave.

"Brave you have never seen my wings. You have only seen them covered over with this jacket."

"Are you sure you want to do this now?" cautioned Bonnie.

"Yes, I'm sure." Irvine reassured her.

Brave gasped, "Dad, you only have one straight wing!"

"Yes, Brave. All my life, I only had one straight wing. My other wing has been bent. I looked different to so many other planes, Brave, that I was afraid what others would say if they saw my wing when I was flying. I didn't want to be treated differently, so I would hide my wing so others wouldn't see that one was bent." explained Irvine.

"But Dad, you are the greatest flier in town!" Brave said.

"But no one knows the truth about my wing, Brave. I know I need to stop hiding it from people." sighed Irvine.

"I know what we will do, Brave..." said Irvine with excitement in his eyes.

"I will teach you to fly! Then we will invite everyone to come and watch us fly together; and I will fly for the first time without my jacket." Irvine said with a smile.

"Wow! Dad, this is a great idea!" applauded Brave.

On that very day, Brave began learning to fly. His dad showed him everything. He would strap Brave to his back and off they would go flying.

He taught him how to take off, how to land, and how to follow a map. He even taught him how to do tricks like loop-de-loop.

A few weeks later Brave was ready for his first flight by himself. He was nervous. His knees began to shake. Irvine was also nervous, but he knew he needed to finally show the world his wings.

They invited the town to the edge of Mount MacBay. Everyone came ready to see Brave fly. Irvine took the stage and nervously spoke. "I know you are all here to see my son fly, but I also wanted to tell you something about me. For years, I have covered my wings because I was afraid of what you would think when you saw them. But today I'm proud to reveal them to you."

Irvine took off his jacket, and there were gasps from the crowd. Some Remarked, "Oooo... look! Is it broken?" Others said,

"That must hurt!" and, "How can he possibly fly like that?"

Irvine continued, "I have always had a bent wing, but I have been able to fly as well as any other plane; and I will no longer hide it from anyone."

The crowd applauded and cheered for Irvine and for Brave.

Brave turned to Irvine, "I'm so proud you are my Dad."

Irvine smiled.
"And I'm so proud of you son. Are you ready to fly?"
"Yes, Dad, I'm ready." beamed Brave.

The crowd counted down, "3-2-1..."
With laughter and joy, Brave and Irvine went
soaring off Mount MacBay.

They both had conquered their fears.

Irvine was no longer afraid to show his wings and they no longer called Brave "the plane who is afraid to fly." He is now known as "Brave, the Bravest!"

Brave MacBay and his father Irvine MacBay both overcame their fears, and so can you. But the key to them winning was by them talking about their fears and no longer hiding them.

QUESTION TO DISCUSS

1) Will Brave ever be afraid to fly again? If he is, what should he do?

2) As a parent, what fears would you be willing to share with your child to help them understand they are not alone?

3) Now that I've shared as a parent some of my fears, what are some fears you have? Encourage your child to share any personal fears that they have.

4) When did you first experience this fear? What did it feel like when you experienced this fear?

5) If you give this fear to God, what do you think He would do with it? Let's give it to Him right now.

Prayer

Father God,

I thank You, for Your word says according to 1 John 4:18,

"There is no fear in love; but perfect love drives out fear."

I ask for Your love to come into the heart of (name child) and for all fear to be driven out by Your love. I ask for Your peace, and comfort to settle over (name child), day and night.

Remind them of Your truth daily.

In Jesus' name,

AMEN.

Printed in the USA
CPSIA information can be obtained
at www.ICGtesting.com
LVHW062135291223
767731LV00015B/104